Release Mrs Terrortoes!

Essex County Council

'Release Mrs Terrortoes!'
An original concept by W. G. White
© W. G. White 2021

Illustrated by Ocean Hughes

Published by MAVERICK ARTS PUBLISHING LTD
Studio 11, City Business Centre, 6 Brighton Road,
Horsham, West Sussex, RH13 5BB
© Maverick Arts Publishing Limited November 2021
+44 (0)1403 256941

A CIP catalogue record for this book is available at the British Library.

ISBN 978-1-84886-842-7

www.maverickbooks.co.uk

This book is rated as: Brown Band (Guided Reading)

Release Mrs Terrortoes!

Written by
W. G. White

Illustrated by
Ocean Hughes

Chapter 1

Joseph could clearly remember the first time he'd met Mrs Terrortoes. He was only three years old at the time, and he'd just received the greatest bed a three-year-old could ask for.

It was brand new, shaped like a rocket, and had astronauts

on the duvet.

Best of all, it was an *actual* bed, not a cot. Finally, Joseph was grown up. It'd been a long three years, but he'd made it.

Unable to contain his excitement, Joseph burst from Dad's arms and dived—headfirst—onto the mattress. It bounced and he squealed with joy.

"Someone's happy." Dad grinned.

"I'm a rocket. Zoom!" Joseph burrowed under the blankets and wiggled to get comfortable. "Nighty sleep," he said.

"Nighty sleep?" Dad laughed. "It's only 3pm, Joseph!"

Joseph pretended to snore.

"Well, I guess I'll have to eat Joseph's dessert tonight," said Dad as he went to the door. "Oh well!"

Joseph almost jumped up. Dessert was the most important meal of the day. Still... his new bed trumped even Dad's homemade apple pie. He kept still, snoring louder and louder until Dad left.

Joseph stopped his snoring and sat upright. He bounced, wiggled, and crawled all over his bed. Exhausted, he laid back and—what was that?

Someone was... snoring? But it wasn't Joseph. This was a deep, terrible snore—like a chugging steam train or Dad! It was coming from underneath the bed! Although he was scared, Joseph knew he couldn't hide under the blankets. He was a big kid now. Big kids were brave.

He slipped onto the floor and got on his hands and knees. It was dark under the bed, but he could see the outline of a lump.

His eyes adjusted and the lump became furry.

The furry lump grew big, floppy ears.

The furry lump with big, floppy ears bounced forward, knocked Joseph onto his back and sat on his chest. It looked like a rabbit crossed with a bear crossed with a pig. It had a wet, twitching nose and a pair of dull tusks sticking out of its bottom jaw.

But most obvious of all was the thing's massive, ridiculous, out-right-silly toes. They were *enormous*! Almost as big as the rest of its body. It twitched those toes as it sat on Joseph's chest. And—although they were terribly big and terribly scary—they were also terribly tickly.

"Stop!" Joseph laugh-cried as he wriggled but the monster didn't stop, and Joseph laughed until he had to roll away.

Joseph and the monster stared at one another.

"You snore loud," said Joseph. "I like you." He sat cross-legged and thought for a moment. His new friend needed a name. "Mrs Edith Terrortoes." He declared. And Edith, with her terribly big toes, did a little hop.

Chapter 2

The years passed one by one and both Joseph and Mrs Edith Terrortoes grew bigger and uglier. Well, Edith got uglier. Joseph looked like a regular boy. A regular boy who'd learned quickly to keep his furry friend a secret from Mum and Dad. Mum and Dad didn't approve of monsters.

Not a lot of people liked monsters. They were noisy and smelly and—sometimes—a bit too playful. Despite monsters being everywhere, people did their best to ignore them.

But not Joseph. Joseph loved Edith. And Edith loved him too. They'd play in his room every night before bed, wrestling, tickling, and racing around. After dark, Joseph would sneak into the kitchen and take a plateful of leftover vegetables for Edith to devour. Edith *adored* day-old Brussels sprouts. The smellier, the better.

At night, when Joseph was snuggled up nice and warm in his bed, Edith would stay up, watching and protecting. She paced the room, searching for intruders or any sort of danger. When she was happy Joseph was safe, she'd squeeze under the bed, curl up, and begin to snore.

It'd been six years since Joseph had discovered Mrs Edith Terrortoes living beneath his bed.

Those snores would strike terror into the hearts of most people but Joseph found them comforting. Edith's snoring was as vital to Joseph as a goodnight's kiss from Mum, or dessert.

Which is why Joseph's world came to a screeching halt when those snores stopped.

Chapter 3

"I saw a Tree Shark yesterday!" Toby exclaimed. Toby was new to the area but he and Joseph had quickly bonded over a shared love of monsters. The boys were walking home from school.

It was a Friday afternoon and Toby was going to stay the night so he could meet Edith. There were few people in the entire world who obsessed over monsters as much as Toby.

"It was all pointy and stuff," said Toby. "Like a hedgehog. I wonder why they don't call them Tree Hogs. Or Hedge Sharks." He was carrying his Book of Monsters, which was basically a list of all known monsters from Big Foot to Nessie. Toby really wanted to identify what sort of monster Edith was.

Joseph didn't mind what sort of monster she was, but didn't see the harm in finding out.

"We're home," Joseph called as he and Toby wandered into the living room, where they found Joseph's parents. Something was wrong. Joseph knew because Dad wasn't wearing his apron. Dad was *always* cooking something.

"Please sit down, Joseph," said Mum. She was still wearing her work suit. Another bad sign.

Joseph and Toby sat on the sofa. A knot was forming in Joseph's stomach and he couldn't untangle it no matter how much he shifted and wiggled.

"This won't be easy to hear," Mum continued softly, "but we found something under your bed."

"A monster," Dad blurted out. "A big, disgusting monster!"

Oh no... Joseph felt like a bucket of ice had been dunked on his head. They'd found Edith!

"Don't be upset, dear," Mum said gently.

Dad forced himself to breathe slowly. "Sorry, they're just so—"

"I was talking to Joseph." Mum crouched and put a hand on Joseph's knee. "We got rid of it, okay? You're perfectly safe. That awful, awful thing can't hurt you any—"

"Edith!" Joseph launched off the sofa and rushed upstairs.

"Joseph!" His mum shouted after him.

Joseph burst into his bedroom, dropped to the floor and looked under the bed. Edith was gone.

"No..." sighed Joseph.

He spent the next half an hour searching his room

from top to bottom. Toby came and helped look, but it was no good. Mrs Edith Terrortoes was nowhere to be seen. The only thing Joseph found was a pamphlet, which read:

Chapter 4

In all his nine years, Joseph had never realised just how dark and spooky his bedroom was at night. The moon shining through the open curtains projected sinister shadows onto his wall. One looked like a reaching claw, whilst another took the shape of a spiky cage. A creak of floorboards set Joseph's heart racing. He clutched his duvet covers up to his nose and shivered. Without Edith's blanket of snoring, Joseph could hear every noise in the entire house, no matter how small.

The **ticking** of his clock drilled into his mind whilst the **clank** and **clang** of pipes in the walls tapped at his imagination. It was much, *much* too quiet.

Nearby, Toby slept on a blow-up mattress. His pyjamas had pictures of all kinds of monsters on them. To Joseph, each one looked like Edith.

What would Lickity and Split, those awful hunters,

be doing to Edith? Was she as scared as Joseph? Was she in pain? He couldn't bear to think about it! Yet... that's all he could do. All night long, Joseph thought of nothing but his friend and how confused and scared she must be feeling.

At the first sign of daylight, Joseph had had enough. He jumped out of bed and shook Toby awake.

"Monsters?" Toby said groggily.

"C'mon, we're getting her back," explained Joseph as he grabbed a backpack and started filling it with clothes and other essentials.

"Get who back?" asked Toby, whose hair was so messy he looked like a monster himself.

Joseph slotted fresh batteries into his megaphone and clipped the cover into place. "Mrs Edith Terrortoes."

Chapter 5

With a bag full of supplies and a mission in mind, Joseph and Toby marched into town. Lickity and Split's address was on the back of their pamphlet, along with drawings of the hunters themselves. They were huge, mountainous men with full beards and perfect smiles.

"Here it is," said Joseph as they arrived at a narrow, rundown building sandwiched between a pet shop and a DIY store.

"I'm gonna record this on my phone," said Toby. "In case we see any rare monsters."

Joseph nodded, pushed the door open, and was surprised by a horrible stench. It was like a poorly managed zoo mixed with an abandoned farm.

Lickity & Split's Really Very Good Monster Hunting Company was dark, moist, and covered in muck. The furniture was wonky, the floor was crooked and even the walls seemed lopsided and uneven.

Just past a pair of rotten doors at the back of the room, Joseph could see cramped cages with sad and uncomfortable monsters stuffed inside. But no sign of Edith.

"I demand the release of Mrs Edith Terrortoes!" shouted Joseph as he stormed up to the welcome desk. Two men lounged on plush rocking chairs behind the desk. One was tall and thin, with narrow rat-like features. The other was plump and round with a squished, squinting face. There wasn't even a chin hair to be shared between them, let alone a full beard.

"D'you 'ear that, Lickity?" said the lanky man with a yellow, bent smirk.

"I do 'ear it, Split," replied the plump man, grinning. "This kid is *demandin'!*"

"That's right!" said Joseph. "She's my friend and you have no right to—"

"No right!" howled Split.

"His friend!" roared Lickity.

The hunters rocked on their chairs, laughing until they had to wipe tears away from their eyes.

"Listen here, you little savage," Lickity snapped. His laughter vanished and was replaced by a mean snarl. "Monsters are nobody's *friend*."

"They're messy beasts," said Split, who unpeeled himself from his chair and towered over Joseph and Toby.

"They're ugly pests," continued Lickity, who'd also managed to roll himself out of his seat.

"They're dangerous animals." Split took a step closer and the boys instinctively moved backwards.

"Stinky brutes." Lickity followed, his feet thundering on the floor.

"Evil plagues." The hunters continued to stalk forward, pushing Joseph and Toby closer and closer to the door.

"Monsters are a lot of things, boys," shouted Lickity as Joseph and Toby were forced back out, onto the street.

"But they're certainly *not friends!*" finished Split, who slammed the door, leaving only cruel laughter ringing in Joseph's ears.

Chapter 6

Well, that went almost exactly as Joseph had expected. Thankfully, he'd come prepared. Within the hour, the boys had created protest signs using supplies from the nearby DIY store, and were chanting, **'Release Mrs Terrortoes!'** over and over. Joseph used his megaphone and managed to draw a small crowd of curious onlookers.

But when people realised the boys were fighting to *help* the monsters, they soon showed their true colours.

"Lock them up and throw away the key," sneered one woman.

"A monster ate my lunch last week," said another, "I hate them all."

"Daft boys," muttered an old man. "We hunt monsters for a reason!"

"Monsters are bad!" people moaned.

"Monsters are messy!" people cried.

"We don't want them!" people declared.

Yet Joseph and Toby continued their protest, knowing that people were wrong. They shouted and demanded for Edith's release, until a small voice cut through the ever-growing rabble of onlookers.

"The monster hunters took my best friend too."

It was a girl, a little younger than Joseph. "He was small and blue and I loved him. And they took him away." She picked up a sign and joined the protest.

Something shifted in the onlookers and it was as if a dam broke. Kids and adults of all shapes and sizes rushed forward in support of the monsters. Some created their own signs, others simply took up the chant.

"Release the monsters! Release the monsters! Release the monsters!"

Before long, the protesters outnumbered the onlookers—and more were arriving from all over town as word spread.

Inside Lickity & Split's Really Very Good Monster Hunting Company, Lickity and Split watched on through a grubby window, with a growing sense of worry.

Chapter 7

When the local news vans arrived, Joseph knew they were starting to make a difference. Before long, national news crews showed up. Then international reporters. Word continued to spread thick and fast as monster supporters joined in from all over the world. People were protesting about monster hunters everywhere from America to Germany, Australia to New Zealand and beyond. Monster lovers of all shapes and sizes shouted together:

Release the monsters!

Meanwhile Joseph and Toby were in for a surprise.

"Woah!" exclaimed Toby as he urgently patted Joseph on the shoulder. "I-It's B-B-B-B—"

"Bruce Alford!" Joseph couldn't believe his eyes. Wading through the protesters, with a string of fans behind him, was the big-time movie star Bruce Alford. He stood head and shoulders above most people, wore big sunglasses and a massive smile, and was heading straight for Joseph.

"Hey there, boys," said Bruce in an American accent. "Love what you're doing. Some pals and I were hoping we could join in?"

"We?" asked Joseph, and Bruce gestured down the street. Someone had rolled out a red carpet and a flock of famous faces were strutting down it, towards the protests.

There were movie stars, singers, models, athletes, TV personalities and more. Joseph didn't know all of them, but he recognised most.

"I can't," said Toby, his whole body shaking and his eyes exploding out of his head. "Celebrities. Everywhere. This is the best. Day. EVER!"

"Welcome aboard," said Joseph, who shook Bruce Alford's hand, and watched as the celebrities lifted signs and added their voices to the chant.

Inside, Lickity and Split had been busy bees. They knew what was coming next, and rather than fight the protests, they prepared for a much bigger threat...

"They're here!" Lickity wailed. "We're not ready! They'll shut us down! They'll—"

"Shut it, will ya? We're fine," Split said, though his shaking hands betrayed his inner feelings.

A knock at the building's rear door sent ice down both men's spines.

When they opened the door they found a bald man in a black suit.

"MI0 Agent David D. Light," the man said as he flashed an ID badge. "I'm sure you know why I'm here."

Chapter 8

The front door to Lickity & Split's Really Very Good Monster Hunting Company burst open and the protest fell silent. Joseph and Toby approached the entrance with the other protestors close behind them.

A man wearing a black suit stepped into the street, cast a cold eye over the crowds, and eventually looked down at the boys. "Agent David D. Light, MI0. I need a word with the ringleader here."

"MI0," Toby gasped. "You're like secret agents but for supernatural things!"

"I can neither confirm nor deny that statement," said D. Light. He removed his sunglasses and met Joseph's eye. "You're the leader, I understand?"

"Those monsters didn't hurt anyone," Joseph said, his arms crossed. "We're not leaving until they're released."

"Let's step inside and discuss your concerns with the owners."

With the triumphant roars of the crowd behind them, Joseph and Toby followed Agent D. Light back into the building... and were shocked by what they saw.

Lickity and Split had been busy indeed. The entire building was cleaned from top to bottom, monsters roamed freely, sniffing at scratching posts, eating merrily, and rolling around in fresh hay. Some were even playing with balls and strings of yarn.

"Edith!" Joseph exclaimed as he spotted Mrs Terrortoes shivering in a sparkling clean corner. He rushed over to the monster and threw his arms around her. Edith did a bark-snort—which Joseph knew to be a happy sound—and nuzzled her snout into his neck.

"See, we don't know what the fuss is about," said Lickity, who was wearing a top hat for some reason. "All the monsters are 'appy enough. We take right good care of 'em!"

"That's a lie!" shouted Joseph. "They had them in tiny cages and this place was horrid!"

"He's just making a fuss," snarled Split. "Regular little brat who doesn't like the word 'no'."

"Everything's meeting official MIO guidelines for monster housing," said D. Light, "and these men have a permit. That means they're allowed to keep pest-like monsters. Unless you can prove they're being mistreated, I have to rule in favour of the hunters."

Joseph was just about ready to scream. Lickity and Split were lying straight to the agent's face. As soon as he left, they'd go back to their old ways of cramming monsters into tiny cages—he knew they would. It wasn't right. But how could he stop it? How could he fix it?

"Toby's recording!" Joseph exclaimed. He snatched Toby's phone, found the recording of their first visit and stuffed the screen in D. Light's face. "We have proof and it's right here."

Agent D. Light watched the video, frowning. "Right then," he said, turning to face a very scared-looking Lickity and Split. "You gentlemen are in trouble..."

Lickity and Split shouted, demanded and eventually begged but it made no difference. Agent D. Light slapped handcuffs around their wrists and led them out of the door, but Joseph wasn't paying attention. He was too busy giving Edith a big, fat hug.

Chapter 9

The world watched on, celebrating as a stream of monsters stampeded out of Lickity & Split's Really Very Good Monster Hunting Company. Some of the creatures fell into the arms of loved ones, whilst others rushed into alleyways or disappeared into sewers. It didn't matter where they went—monsters could look after themselves—it only mattered that they were free.

Joseph waved goodbye to Toby, who was busy speaking excitedly with the news crews and celebrities. He had a small gang of little monsters twisting around his feet. It seemed Toby had made some monster friends of his own.

Back home, Joseph wrestled with Edith. They laughed, tickled, played, and eventually fell asleep together.

"I don't understand," Dad whispered to Mum as they watched Joseph and Edith sleeping. "She's just so... *monstrous*."

"Maybe," said Mum, "but she makes Joseph happy." They closed the door, leaving Joseph and Edith to their shared slumber.

Edith's snoring was loud and thunderous that night, like a chugging steam train or Dad. To Joseph, those snores were a second blanket. They were vital. And he'd never be without them again.

Discussion Points

1. Where did Joseph find Mrs Terrortoes at the beginning of the story?

2. What does Edith do that helps Joseph feel safe and sleepy?
a) She runs around
b) She snores
c) She hides in the wardrobe

3. What was your favourite part of the story?

4. How did Joseph and Toby prove that Lickety and Split were lying?

5. Why do you think some people liked monsters?

6. Who was your favourite character and why?

7. There were moments in the story when Joseph decided to **take action for a cause**. Where do you think the story shows this most?

8. What do you think happens after the end of the story?

Book Bands for Guided Reading

The Institute of Education book banding system is a scale of colours that reflects the various levels of reading difficulty. The bands are assigned by taking into account the content, the language style, the layout and phonics. Word, phrase and sentence level work is also taken into consideration.

The Maverick Readers Scheme is a bright, attractive range of books covering the pink to grey bands. All of these books have been book banded for guided reading to the industry standard and edited by a leading educational consultant.

To view the whole Maverick Readers scheme, visit our website at

www.maverickearlyreaders.com

Or scan the QR code to view our scheme instantly!

Maverick Chapter Readers
(From Lime to Grey Band)

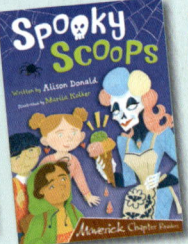